The Worst Football Team

Martin Smith

Illustrated by

Philip Knibbs

ISBN: 978-1-7395373-0-2

For Bradshaw

Contents

Acknowledgments

Many children's books feature football super stars and famous players.

Fair enough, they are the best in the world.

But what about everyone else?

Every Saturday and Sunday, millions of people play or watch football.

Where are their stories?

This book is for them.

It is for everyone outside the Premier League.

This will be a perfect read if you're a child who likes football.

And if you're a grown-up who likes to read with the kids, this is kind of aimed at you too.

It's not only words.

The Meerkats have been brought to life brilliantly by the incredibly talented Phil Knibbs.

Thanks go to numerous other people who helped me.

Football expert and Newcastle United fan Mark Newnham created the brilliantly vivid cover.

Veteran sports hack Alan Poole provided an expert eye to keep the story on track while Richard Wayte did his usual proofreading masterclass to ensure my excited storytelling made sense.

And finally, thank you for reading.

Oh, and always, always believe.

1. WELCOME

Close your eyes. No, really close them. No peeking. That's better.

Imagine yourself scoring a great goal.

There's a football at your feet. With a single kick, you smash it perfectly into the top corner.

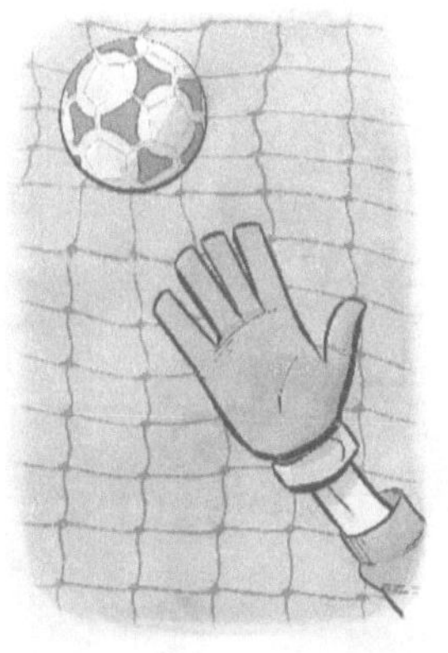

GOAL!

The net bulges. The crowd goes wild. You've won the World Cup.

You are a hero. Your arms go up and you do a cool celebration dance with the rest of the team.

The fans sing your name. Everyone thinks you're ace.

A football superstar. A football genius.

Lane Meerkats Under-7s players are no different. They have that dream too.

They have the same thoughts (apart from a member of the team who only thinks about spiders).

Yet in their dreams, they miss the ball. Or the goal.

Sometimes they miss both.

This is because Meercats' players can't play football.

This sounds horrid. It's not. Trust me. I'm being nice when I say that.

They are much, much worse than I can ever tell you.

Meerkats have been training for a whole year.

But the truth is simple: they're clueless about soccer.

Rubbish. Hopeless. Terrible.

Somehow, the Meerkats players don't know this.

They think they're going to win the World Cup.

They haven't even worked out yet they can't enter the World Cup.

Billions of people watch football on television each week.

Millions attend matches every weekend. Hundreds of thousands play soccer on a Saturday.

Thousands of managers complain on the touchline whenever they get a chance.

Hundreds of scouts trawl the country looking for the best talent.

Only seven players can say proudly that they play for Lane FC Meerkats Under-7s. And that's more than enough.

To be fair, they are unbeaten – because they haven't had a match yet.

But the team – and absolutely no one else – believes they are ready for the next step.

No one can say Meerkats don't care.

They turn up to training every week.

Sometimes they listen to Coach Mark too.

Occasionally, they even manage to kick the ball in the right direction.

And they are certain that one day, their footballing dreams will come true.

This is that journey. Kind of.

2. MEERKATS

Come a bit closer. Let me share a little secret with you.

Every soccer team in the world needs players. I know, I know. It's not the best secret – I did say it was only a little secret – mainly because everyone knows this already.

But the truth is you need to have players to have a game of football.

Great footballers make the best teams.

Think of the world's most famous clubs. Barcelona. Real Madrid. Bayern Munich. Everton.

Or the countries that are great at football.

Brazil. England. France. Argentina.

Your best players can make the difference between winning and losing.

They score goals when all hope is lost. They tackle when their tired legs feel like wobbly jelly.

Or make an incredible save from nowhere.

Meerkats U7s have players.

Seven of them.

They even have enough for one of them to be a substitute.

They are improving every week at training. In fact, they almost know each other's names now.

This is the good news.

Meerkats players are … different to the football greats.

For starters, they're only six or seven years old. And most of them haven't got a clue about the famous teams we've just mentioned.

You're going to meet them – and their coach – in a minute.

Promise you won't laugh?

They love football. And rules. And spiders. And getting muddy. And talking about poop.

Sometimes they talk all the time. On other days, no one speaks. They're like that.

This is a story about football.

And it's as far away from the bright lights of football as you can get.

If you're reading this hoping to discover the next Football Boy Wonder, then that's a different story.

This is about the worst football team in the world.

3. THE COACH

Football coaches come in all shapes and sizes.

Thin like a pencil.

Round like a blubbery walrus.

Hairy as a badger.

Or as bald as an eel.

They can look like ANYTHING.

But some facts about football coaches apply to every one of them.

Everyone who runs a kids' football team is old and grumpy.

That's the only qualifications you need to be a football coach.

The test for a coach is pretty easy.

Imagine you want to be a football coach.

You sit down at a small table.

There is a piece of paper in front of you with two questions on it:

1. Are you grumpy? Yes or No?

2. Are you old? Yes or No?

If you answer 'yes' to both, then you can be a football coach.

It's that simple. If – somehow – you get the answers wrong, you can always go back and do it again.

Coach Mark is the coach for Lane FC Meerkats Under-7s.

He is ancient (perhaps 40) and has a beard.

Coach Mark loves football.

Although you wouldn't always know it. He can be unhappy. And that's being polite.

Wiping Brendan's bogies off the training footballs does not please Coach Mark.

Nor does talking about spiders.

Or hogging the ball.

In fact, Coach Mark can get cross at A LOT of things.

He is an extremely nice man. You'll meet him in a moment.

Luckily, Coach Mark has been training Meerkats for a long time and soon they will be ready for matches.

There is still work to be done but Coach Mark has drawn up a list of the team's strengths:

- PASSING – the team cannot do this

- BALL CONTROL – Dribbler can dribble. No one else can

- SHOOTING – Coach Mark forbids toe pokes ... so the entire team cannot shoot

- TACKLING – there was one attempt at learning how to tackle. Coach Mark has banned any mention of that terrible day ever since

- GOALKEEPING – no one has managed a catch yet, but several players refused to let go of the ball when they picked it up off the floor

- FITNESS – Coach Mark cancelled the session after six minutes, blaming a headache.

But training has helped.

The Meerkats can run. Fast, too.

To be truthful, they can't all run at the same time in the right direction, but that's next on the list.

In other good news:

- They pretty much know everyone's names

- Thanks to Stevie, they know loads about spiders

- They are sensible enough to only use the training balls not covered in Brendan's bogies.

Coach Mark can take the credit for these amazing steps forward.

He is certain the team is improving.

You or I would probably disagree.

They're terrible.

But Coach Mark says he is happy.

It is hard to tell if he is happy.

It's probably the beard. Or the frown. Who knows?

If players win games, it is only because their coaches tell them to.

Luckily, Meerkats have Coach Mark.

4. MEET THE TEAM

Name: Coach Mark

Age: Very, very old

Position: On the sideline

Likes: Rules, shouting, beards, being grumpy, bad music, pretending to be a DJ

Dislikes: Everything else

Coach Mark runs Lane FC Meerkats Under-7s.

He organises training every week, puts out lots of cones and has a whistle.

Coach Mark is kind. And very patient.

But this team could drive anyone crazy.

He is busy preparing for the team's big match – their first-ever league game.

Name: Pellie

Age: 7

Position: Goalkeeper

Likes: Cereal sandwiches, the sea, Christmas, Hildy

Dislikes: Her name, mum,

Pellie is the team's captain and goalkeeper. Coach Mark made Pellie the goalkeeper because she's the tallest player on the team.

Pellie did not want to be goalkeeper but did not complain either.

She has other things to think about.

Mainly, she thinks her name is horrible. She is convinced Pellie is not even a real name.

Her mum says Pellie IS a real name and she must stop being silly. They talk about this EVERY DAY.

Pellie does not like her mum.

Name: Dazza

Age: 7

Position: Defender

Likes: Football, especially Lane FC, television, video games

Dislikes: Running, talking, being outside, whistles, fitness

Dazza loves football. He watches it every day. He collects soccer stickers. He drinks out of a water bottle like Premier League superstars.

Dazza is the happiest player on the team. He is giddy even thinking about playing for Lane FC. He can't sleep because he gets too excited.

But Dazza doesn't exercise. He sits all day and watches the telly. Or plays football video games.

LANE MEERKATS FC

DAZZA

So, his dad signed him up to get him fit. And it's not going very well.

If Dazza can play for longer than two minutes and not fall asleep in the match, he will shock everyone.

Name: Stevie

Age: 6

Position: Defender

Likes: Spiders, books about spiders, videos about spiders, bow ties

Dislikes: Dirt, Coach Mark, football, anyone who doesn't love spiders

Stevie thinks football is strange. He only plays because his sister Kazzie is in Lane FC's Under-9s.

Stevie always carries a spider book with him. Spiders are his favourite.

Coach Mark says books are not allowed during training and matches. He is strict on this. This annoys Stevie.

Every week Stevie leaves his book on the touchline, along with a water bottle and bow tie. No one asks

about the bow tie and Stevie does not tell anyone either.

Stevie and Coach Mark fall out every week – mainly over the book and Stevie's questions about spiders.

Name: Bolo

Age: 7

Position: Midfielder

Likes: Spaceships, football, swapping stickers

Dislikes: People who foul, oranges, dancing

Bolo's real name is not Bolo. It's Bo Long. But everyone calls him Bolo.

Bolo, who wants to be a space ranger when he grows up, has been part of Meercats for almost a year.

And he is getting better.

Last week he nearly touched the ball in a training match.

It was so close – the ball whizzed over his foot and it had gone before he realised it was there.

It was a moment he would never forget. The team had celebrated like he scored a hat trick.

Bolo likes football but playing tag during Coach Mark's warm-up is his number one.

Name: Hildy

Position: Midfielder

Age 7.

Likes: Coach Mark, ballet, being muddy, Christmas, tackling, Pellie

Dislikes: Pellie's name, losing, arguing

Hildy loves ballet. But her mum insists she gets fresh air once a week so she comes to Meerkats.

Hildy doesn't mind football but she prefers Christmas.

She doesn't understand the rules but loves sliding on wet mud. You're not allowed to be muddy in ballet so playing football is great.

Hildy loves to tackle people. Sometimes on the pitch, sometimes off it.

LANE MEERKATS FC

HILDY

She thinks Coach Mark is ace. He's very kind and caring, unlike her horrible dance teachers.

Hildy is best friends with Pellie. She thinks Pellie's name is silly too.

Name: Dribbler

Position: Striker.

Age: 6.

Likes: Football, scoring goals, beating players

Dislikes: Passing, defending

Dribbler has been playing football since he was two and joined Lane FC when he was four.

His dad tells anyone who will listen that his boy is going to be a Premier League star.

He is small but super quick.

Dribbler is good. Everyone knows he is the best player on the team.

He is the only member of Meercats who can run with the ball.

He is also the only one who shoots with power.

But he never passes or defends.

This makes Coach Mark mad.

Brendan

Age: 6

Position: Substitute

Likes: Giggling, looking at birds in the sky, picking his nose, running

Dislikes: Spiders, custard, training bibs

Brendan turns up to training every week.

He was the first one to start training and has made the least progress. An impressive feat. This is because he keeps the same routine.

He stays quiet most of the time and picks his nose, no matter who is looking.

Then he wipes the bogies on his shirt. Or the training balls.

Brendan does not dribble or pass the ball. He simply wellies it away when it's anywhere near him.

Every session, Coach Mark tells him not to do this. Brendan does not listen. This is repeated every week.

5. TRAINING

Every Wednesday, Lane Meerkats' players train for an hour.

Several teams train on the Lane FC pitches at the same time.

Next to the Meerkat are the Under-15s team, the Panthers.

They are all HUGE.

Their coach is a man called JP. He is super mean, and a lot angrier than Coach Mark.

The Meerkats try to stay as far away as possible from JP and his team of giants.

If one of the Meerkat's footballs accidentally strays into the Under-15s part of the pitch, JP shouts at anyone nearby.

And I mean ANYONE.

Coach Mark. Meerkats.

The Under-15s.

The parents watching. The poor groundsman.

One time an unlucky ice cream van was on the wrong end of a JP terrible tongue-lashing.

Coach Mark is not mad enough to stand up to JP. But he is clever enough to try to stop this from happening.

He plans training carefully every week. He encourages the team to pass the ball and shoot with power – at the opposite end of the pitch away from JP and his team.

Sadly, none of the team can pass or shoot yet. But they are getting better. After a year of learning, every member of Meerkats now stays on their part of the pitch for almost the entire session.

Stevie no longer takes a book onto the pitch.

Hildy doesn't do ballet routines during the warm-up any more.

Remarkably, Dazza hasn't fallen asleep in the session for weeks.

Things are looking up.

The Meerkats are on a roll.

Today's training is important.

There are only three training sessions before Meerkats' first-ever game.

Coach Mark is the first to arrive.

They train in a small field behind Lane FC's main pitch.

The training pitches are bumpy with lots of cracks.

There is a large clump of bushes behind one end. If someone whacks a shot hard enough, they have to go into the bushes to get the ball back.

This has not happened to the Meerkats yet.

Coach Mark has a set routine.

He always gets there early to set up. He carries a small goal to the area where the team trains.

He puts the footballs out and then lays out the cones for the night's training session.

Today is no different.

Dazza is the first player to arrive, wearing the latest United shirt. He has a new kit every month.

He has not decided what team to support yet.

"Hello Dazza."

"Hi Coach Mark. Am I first here?"

Dazza was always early.

"Yes, you are, buddy. Get practising. The big game will be here soon."

Coach Mark throws him a ball, which Dazza misses.

Coach Mark turns and sees Stevie, sitting next to the pitch.

He is reading a book about spiders.

Stevie always wears a red bow tie to training. No one is quite sure why.

Today the bow tie is wrapped around his head like a headband. He looks like a Christmas present.

Coach Mark ignores the bow tie.

"Hi Stevie.

"Do you want to put the book down and come with Dazza to warm up?"

No answer. Coach Mark moves closer.

"Stevie?"

Steve does not look up. He checks his watch instead.

"Fourteen more minutes."

Then Stevie's eyes return to the spider book.

Coach Mark is confused. He checks his phone. Stevie is correct – the time is 5.46pm. Training will start in 14 minutes.

He tries one more time.

"Do you fancy starting warming up a little earlier? Getting some extra practise will help you loads in the future."

Stevie does not reply.

Coach Mark already knows the answer. He gives up.

In the meantime, Dribbler has arrived, weaving in and out of the cones with his special ball.

He does not say hello either.

Dazza, red-faced and out of breath, stands nearby. He has the ball back.

But he does not want to chase after his ball again so he holds it under his arm and watches Dribbler instead.

"HI COACH MARK!"

Bolo and Pellie arrive together.

They are always excited whenever they see Coach Mark.

"Hi Bolo. Hi Pellie. Grab a ball. Let's get moving."

"THANKS COACH MARK!"

They both pick up a ball and run on to the pitch with big smiles.

"Coach Mark. A word, please."

Coach Mark knows that voice.

Hildy and her mum Martha are standing behind him.

Martha looks angry.

Her giant dog Bonnie looks like a small bear and is staring at the footballs nearby.

There is a little bit of drool coming from the dog's mouth.

Martha shrieks: "We had disgraceful scenes outside our house this week.

"And she says … YOU … told her to do it!"

Silence.

Everyone stares at Mum Martha.

She looks like a firework the moment before it explodes.

Mum points at Hildy.

"She wiped out the postman! With two feet! Not a ball in sight.

"The poor woman has been unable to walk without a limp since!"

Hildy's smile is now as wide as a river.

You know, the type of river where zebras splash around and try to dodge crocodiles.

It's THAT big.

Before Coach Mark can reply, Hildy pipes up: "Yes, he did, Mumma!

"He wanted us to practise tackling. I did exactly as Coach Mark asked us to do last week."

Coach Mark groans.

He's had this problem with Hildy before.

The last time it was a paperboy, with an injured ankle.

He says gently: "Hildy, thank you for listening.

"I'm glad you like to tackle. It's important in football to tackle opposition players.

"However, tackling the postie when she delivers letters to your house is not cool.

"Please don't do that again."

Hildy sees Pellie wandering over. She gives Coach Mark the thumbs up and shoots over to her friend.

Mum Martha gives Coach Mark another scowl and walks off.

Coach Mark checks his watch.

It's 6.03pm. They are late.

Stevie is still reading.

Brendan has arrived silently.

He is now standing in the goal, with a finger jammed up his nose.

Hildy and Pellie are whispering and giggling together.

Bolo is chasing Dribbler with little luck. Dazza is yawning.

Coach Mark blows the whistle.

Training has begun.

6. FITNESS

The Meerkats surround Coach Mark.

Coach Mark said: "Hiya Meerkats.

"Right, it's a really simple start, gang.

"We need to get much fitter so today we're going to do some fitness training.

"When I blow my whistle, I want you to run as fast as you can to the row of cones over there and then back."

Coach Mark points to the row of blue cones about 20 metres away.

Hildy looks. Pellie looks. Dazza looks.

Stevie gazes sadly at the book sitting on the touchline.

No one else bothers.

Coach Mark blows the whistle.

"Go!"

Bolo and Dribbler shoot off at top speed.

Brendan and Stevie don't move.

Dazza takes a step, grabs his arm, rolls on the floor and shouts that he's hurt his leg.

Hildy and Pellie jog to the blue cones and back without any fuss.

But Bolo and Dribbler have gone.

They dash straight past the blue cones.

Coach Mark shouts: "Come back!

"You've gone too far!"

But Bolo and Dribbler are not listening.

It is neck and neck.

They are running so fast that they feel like their legs can't keep up.

They run straight out of the Meerkats training area.

This is bad.

Coach Mark's cheeks turn red.

He shouts: "COME BACK NOW!"

No answer. They keep going.

The boys fly into JP's training area without noticing – and keep running at full pelt.

They are not stopping. Coach Mark gasps. This is worse than bad.

He looks towards the Under-15s in the far corner of the pitch.

Luckily, JP has his back turned to the intruders and has not seen them.

Coach Mark puts a hand over his eyes.

There's a set of blue cones … at the far end of the pitch.

They are almost impossible to see but, somehow, the boys are running towards them.

Bolo and Dribbler are still running flat out, side-by-side.

"OI! YOU TWO!"

Disaster. JP has seen them.

His shout is loud enough to shatter windows.

Even Bolo and Dribbler hear him.

Coach Mark rushes towards JP who is now charging to the boys.

Immediately, Bolo and Dribbler change course – running at full speed for the exit.

Eyes down, this is no longer a competition to see who is the best runner. This is a race for survival.

JP takes off after them.

He can run quicker than a baboon with a stolen box of chocolates.

Coach Mark chases JP.

All of them head towards the gap in the hedge, which leads to the football club's gate.

The rest of the Meerkats are left alone.

Brendan picks his nose.

Stevie is happily sitting cross-legged on the floor, reading his book about spiders.

Dazza is still lying on the ground, enjoying the unexpected break.

Pellie and Hildy look around at the rest of the team.

"See you next week," they say to each other.

7. POOP

Coach Mark stands in front of the Meerkats. This is the last but one training session before the big match. It is VERY important.

For once, everyone is there on time.

Coach Mark is pleased.

"Well done everybody for being ready to play on time. Great stuff."

Dazza finishes a chocolate bar, burps and holds his stomach with both hands.

Coach Mark ignores Dazza.

Instead, he waves his arms.

"This is our part of the field. This is the ONLY area we are allowed in when training. We are not allowed ANYWHERE else."

He points over to where the Under-15s play.

There is a small plastic fence dividing the two playing areas.

JP is staring across the fence.

He is turning purple across his cheeks and his foot is pawing the ground like an angry bull.

The Meerkats turn away, quickly.

Several of the team begin to shuffle towards the corner, trying to get away from JP and his evil glare.

Coach Mark blows his whistle.

The Meerkats look at him. Dazza burps.

Coach Mark ignores him – again.

"Today we are going to practise shooting. Pellie needs to practise saving the ball.

"And the rest of you need to learn to shoot with power. Any questions?"

Dazza's hand shoots up.

"I don't feel well, Coach Mark."

The rest of the Meerkats take a step away from Dazza, who has turned a funny shade of red.

Then they realise they've moved closer to JP and his evil glare – and quickly step back.

Coach Mark thinks quickly.

"Dazza, what's wrong? You don't look well."

Dazza groans: "It might have been the hotdogs. Or the pasta. It definitely wasn't the crisps. Or the chocolate bar.

"But it could have been the strawberry milkshake. Or the chicken nuggets."

Coach Mark scratches his head.

"You've eaten all that … today?"

"No, for tea.

"About 20 minutes ago. I need to go to the toilet, Coach Mark."

"Wow."

For a moment, Coach Mark is lost for words.

"I see … OK, Dazza. No problem. You know where the loo is."

Dazza has one hand gripping his tummy and the other wrapped around his bum.

He is out of breath, even though he's standing still. It is a strange sight.

It looks like he is trying to ballroom dance with himself.

He pleads: "No.

"I can't make it that far. I need to go pooper, Coach Mark. I need to go soon. Noooooooooow!"

Coach Mark has never heard the word 'pooper' before.

He tries to be calm.

"OK, go for a wee behind the bushes in the halfway line."

Dazza looks like he might explode: "But I need more than a wee. I need to do a massive …"

"Okay, Dazza, we get it," Coach Mark interrupts.

"Can you make it to the toilet?"

"No."

"Can you hold on until the end of the session?"

"No way."

"Ok, the bushes are the only option. Don't worry we'll start training and you can catch up."

Dazza waddles towards the bushes, still holding his bum.

Coach Mark turns to the rest of the Meerkats.

"Any other questions that do not involve poo – or spiders?"

Stevie looks mad. Hildy's hand goes up.

"Yes, Hildy," says Coach Mark.

"Coach Mark, why are you wearing sunglasses when it's raining?"

All the Meerkats stare at Coach Mark.

Hildy is right. He IS wearing sunglasses in the rain.

This is strange.

The Meerkats rarely ask questions that do not involve spiders.

But when Coach Mark wears sunglasses in the rain, that changes completely.

"Are you trying to develop night vision, Coach Mark?"

"Do you want to be a rock and roll star, Coach Mark?"

"Do you have mini windscreen wipers on them to get rid of the rain, Coach Mark?"

"Why do you like sunglasses but hate spiders, Coach Mark?"

Coach Mark ignores all questions and marches towards the goal.

Pellie pulls her new goalkeeping gloves on.

They've not been used yet despite being brought to the last six training sessions.

"Ow … ouch … arrggghhh."

Dazza does not like thorns.

The team moves towards the balls while listening to Dazza's cries.

Stevie usually leaves his bow tie on the sidelines but not today.

He straightens the tie before running up to shoot.

Before Stevie can reach the ball, a voice pops out of the hedge.

"COACH MARK?"

"Yes, Dazza?"

"I've done it. It's a whopper."

"Well done. Fancy coming and joining us?"

"I haven't got any tissue to wipe up."

Coach Mark rolls his eyes.

"Well, I can't help...."

"I'VE GOT SOME!"

Before Coach Mark can say anything, Hildy bounds towards the gap through the bushes waving a small tissue in front of her.

"I'M COMING!"

Hildy disappears out of sight.

Coach Mark turns back to training.

Stevie runs up and boots the ball with all his might.

It does not have enough power to reach Pellie's goal but Stevie seems happy.

Coach Mark is kind.

"Well done, Stevie.

"That would have been on target.

"Next time, give it a little more welly."

Pellie scoops the ball up and chucks it at Stevie's head.

He ducks and it misses him.

However, he somehow manages to knock his bow tie off.

Stevie howls like he's been hit and dives to pick up the bow tie.

Pellie puts her hands up in the air.

"Didn't touch him, Boss. Honest."

Coach Mark walks forward.

"Stevie...."

He is interrupted by a rumpus coming from the bushes.

"OH MY GOD. THAT IS DISGUSTING. …"

Coach Mark spins around at the sound of Hildy's voice.

Everyone looks at the bushes.

"BLARGHHH … THAT IS HORRIBLE…. BLARGHHH!"

Coach Mark scratches his head.

Bolo runs up the take the next shot.

He misses the ball completely.

BLARGHHHH!

"Next," shouts Pellie with a yawn.

Coach Mark is still looking at the hedgerow.

Brendan toe-punts the ball five metres wide.

BLARGHHHH!

Pellie sighs.

"Next."

Deep in the bushes, Dazza's voice pipes up. "Coach Mark, come quick! Hildy's not feeling well!"

BLARGHHH!

"Coach Mark! Hildy is REALLY poorly. She can't stand up. You've gotta help her!"

Coach Mark puffs out his cheeks.

"Stay here," he tells the rest of the Meerkats. "I'll be back in a second."

Dribbler lines up to take the next shot.

He runs to the ball, controls it and runs directly at the goal.

"That's not SHOOTING!" screams Pellie.

Dribbler does not care.

He dribbles – he doesn't waste time shooting.

He takes the ball around a furious Pellie, dribbles behind the goal and returns the ball to the starting point.

Bolo and Brendan clap. Dribbler
bows.

Pellie looks mad. Coach Mark
ignores them. Instead, he walks
towards the hedge to find the two
missing Meerkats players.

"HEADS UP!"

A ball flies over their heads and crashes into the bushes.

The Meerkats look around in shock.

None of them can kick it that high.

They are much bigger balls than the ones they use.

A gruff voice barks out. "I'll get it."

JP does not give the Meerkats a second glance.

He brushes rudely past Coach Mark without speaking.

JP charges into the hedge, crashing through branches and thorns.

"OWWW!"

"Dazza? Are you OK?" asks Coach Mark.

"This stupid ball fell out of the tree and…."

Dazza stops talking as JP finds them.

"What the hell is going … owww …
WHAT'S THIS?!"

Hildy shouts: "Coach Mark, help!"

Coach Mark looks alarmed. He makes up his mind. He has to go in there as well. Coach Mark takes a deep breath and follows JP's tracks. Seconds later, he is out of sight.

But then something very strange starts happening.

The whole bush is trembling.

It's like a giant is inside the hedge, shaking it from top to bottom.

The Meerkats are transfixed as leaves and twigs fall from the vibrating bushes. It's completely silent on the training pitch.

Even the Under-15s have stopped training to watch the hedge.

It is most unusual, to be fair.

Normally, no one spends any time in the hedge. Today is different.

Two coaches, two players and a football are in there – at the same time. The rustling deep inside the hedge goes into overdrive.

And then … JP appears holding the ball. He looks angrier and more red-faced than ever. The Meerkats gasp in shock. JP scowls at them in silence. His blue tracksuit is smothered in runny brown POOP.

There are white and orange lumps of SICK in his hair. A mixture of brown and white dribbles down his chubby cheek.

JP's eyes look wild. He staggers onto the training pitch. JP can't speak.

He is too shocked. And he smells really bad. Like worn socks.

Which have been dipped in eggs.

And left in the rain for three days.

And been puked up by a dog.

JP is furious. He's so cross, he looks like he might EXPLODE at any moment.

There is no sign or sound of Coach Mark, Dazza or Hildy. This is bad.

"RUN!"

Pellie is the first to scarper.

The rest of the Meerkats follow.

They dash off before JP erupts.

Training is over for another week.

8. TACTICS

Today's training is special.

It is the final session before the Meerkats' first-ever match.

It has been decided Meerkats should not train anywhere near JP or his Under-15s team this week.

Instead, Coach Mark has arranged to meet at 4pm in the Lane FC clubhouse.

He has not told the team why they are not training in their usual place.

The Meerkats already know the reason – they have a big game so they are now IMPORTANT footballers. This meeting is exciting.

Every member of the team has been given a drink and grapes to eat.

That's how great it is. The Meerkats are sitting on three large settees.

Coach Mark stands in front of them and says they are going to talk about tactics. This sounds brilliant.

Pellie is certain Coach Mark wants to discuss small sweets.

Bolo knows tactics are a game involving skipping.

Dribbler thinks tactics grow on dogs.

Stevie is certain that tactics have nothing to do with spiders.

Hildy's convinced tactics are used to pin posters on walls.

Dazza is disappointed with the grapes. He likes chocolate.

Brendan sits on his hands to stop touching his nose.

Coach Mark has a whiteboard and everything. This is a VERY important meeting.

Pellie waits patiently for the tactics sweets to be shared out. Nothing so far.

Coach Mark starts with a simple fact.

"Welcome Meerkats. This is the last time we'll see each other before the big game on Saturday."

This is TRUE.

Bolo drops a grape in shock.

Dazza scrunches up his empty grape bag, hoping he's missed one.

Coach Mark continues: "Put your book down, Stevie, please."

Stevie gives Coach Mark an evil look.

He keeps reading.

Coach Mark ignores this.

He continues: "We're playing six a side."

Hildy checks her watch.

She puts up her hand to ask a question at the same time as she asks the question.

"Why are we here now if we're playing at six?"

"I won't have time for tea. Shall we come back later?"

Brendan nods.

"Yes, Hildy is right. It will be colder at six. I'd rather play in the morning."

Coach Mark replies gently: "That's good to know. Thankfully you'll be playing in the morning on Saturday."

Bolo looks stunned.

"Six o'clock … in the MORNING? Coach Mark, this is crazy. My alarm doesn't go off until 7.37am. I'm going to be late for our first-ever match."

The whole team look worried now.

Even Stevie looks up from his book.

Coach Mark smiles again, although this time it looks false.

"You will play in the morning, Bolo.

"Our game will kick off at 10.30am."

Dribbler claps his hands together.

 "Excellent. Who is playing at 6pm tonight then? Can we watch them after this meeting about tick-tacks?"

Coach Mark bites his lip.

He is a patient man. "NO! No one is playing tonight.

"We are playing at 10.30am. I meant we are playing six a side."

The team go quiet. This is BIG news. This time Pellie's hand shoots up. Like Hildy, she blurts out the questions straight away. And she has A LOT of questions.

"So, we're playing on the side? This is amazing. It'll be like two games happening at the same time.

"Won't that be confusing? Who is playing on the main pitch then?"

Coach Mark's smile seems to be frozen. He can talk but his lips are barely moving. It's a little weird.

"No, no, no. You're on the pitch. I'm on the side."

Dribbler itches his nose in confusion.

He said: "You're playing too, Coach Mark? Is that allowed?

"You don't see many coaches on the pitch in the Premier League unless they're really angry."

Coach Mark takes a deep breath before replying.

"No, I'm not playing. I am...."

Dribbler interrupts: "But Coach, you said there are six of …

Coach Mark is delighted: "Correct! At last, we're finally getting it."

Dribbler continues: "… me. But there's only one of me."

Coach Mark no longer looks happy.

He looks tired instead.

"No. All of us."

Dazza scratches his head: "So, there are six of all of us?

"Like six times six?

"When do the rest arrive? We're going to have loads of players!"

Brendan: "17 of us?"

Coach Mark: "No."

Hildy guesses: "24?"

Coach Mark: "No."

Stevie, still looking at his book, mutters: "36."

Coach Mark: "Yes."

Bolo: "Wow, 36 players in our team. We're going to be awesome."

Coach Mark: "Yes, Stevie's maths is correct.

"But it has nothing to do with the match.

"There's only going to be six of you playing."

Pellie looks unhappy at this.

She said: "Why are you taking our players away?

"You're making it unfair on us."

Coach Mark tries to interrupt: "I'm not. I...."

Pellie continues: "We could have 36 players. Instead, you decided to have six.

I don't think you're a good manager. You need to go on more coaching courses."

Coach Mark's face turns pale. Pellie stops talking.

Coach Mark speaks quietly but loud enough for everyone to hear.

"This session is going to finish early. We're done. I will see you at 10am tomorrow for warm-up. This is important – DO NOT BE LATE."

9. WARM UP

Apart from Dazza, everyone is late for the warm-up.

Bolo, Dribbler and Stevie arrive only two minutes before kick-off.

Coach Mark is mad. He is not smiling today.

The other team – Foxley Sheepdogs U7s – have been warming up for 30 minutes solid.

They can pass, shoot and tackle.

They have a bright green kit.

Most of them have flash boots without laces.

Coach Mark tries to ignore them.

Meerkats watch them and applaud every time they score a goal, which happens A LOT.

He calls the Meerkats together and reads out the team from his whiteboard.

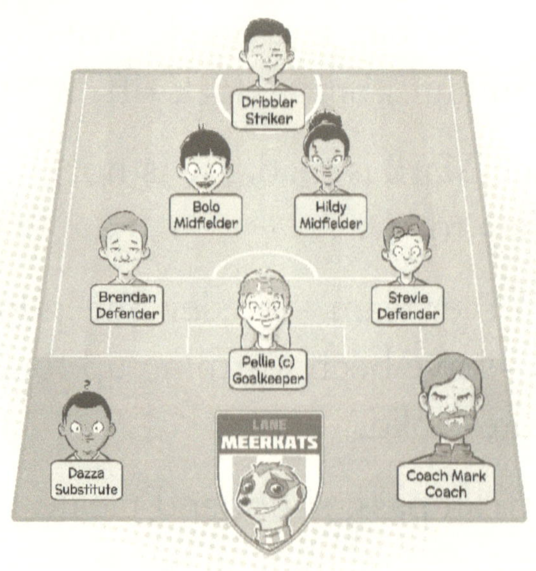

Dazza is crying. "I am a sub because I needed to poop! It's not fair."

Hildy puts an arm around him.

"Don't worry, Dazza. You'll play soon. I know it."

Dazza stops crying.

"Thanks, Hildy. Coach Mark isn't playing the team's best player because of my belchy bottom."

Hildy moves away quickly.

Coach Mark hands out the team's new kit and brings the Meerkats together for a final team talk.

"Right, you lot. Go out there and try your best. Tackle all the time.

"You've worked really hard for this. Go and give it your best shot.

"One final thing – today's captain is going to be ..."

Everyone stays quiet. Coach Mark was almost certain they did not know what a captain did, but was pleased with the moment of peace.

"... Pellie."

He held out an armband with a large 'C' on it.

"Thank you, Coach Mark."

Pellie does not look pleased. She puts the armband around her head. There is no time to say she's wearing the ARMband wrongly.

"Good luck," Coach Mark says.

The team wander onto the pitch, looking thoroughly lost.

"Have you got anything to eat, Coach Mark?" asks Dazza.

10. FIRST HALF

One minute: 1–0 to the Sheepdogs.

Three mins: 4–0.

Six mins: Pellie's mum tells Pellie she should not be wearing the armband around her head. Pellie does not like her mum or her name. And now she doesn't like the armband. She refuses to take it off.

Nine mins: 8–0.

10 mins: Dazza goes on for Brendan.

11 mins: Dazza comes off with a foot injury. Brendan goes back on.

12 mins: 11–0.

14 mins: Stevie asks to be substituted. Coach Mark refuses, knowing Stevie wants to read his spider book.

15 mins: 16–0.

16 mins: The crowd roars as Dribbler takes the ball into the Sheepdogs' half for the first time.

Dribbler goes past one Sheepdogs player. Then a second. And a third.

Suddenly, he's clean through.

Parents gasp.

The moment has arrived. Meerkats' first-ever goal is about to be scored.

But Dribbler does not go for goal.

Head down, he runs straight off the pitch near the corner flag.

He only stops when he gets near the hedge where Dazza had to … well, you know.

The ball trickles into the hedge but Dribbler is already moving backwards, away from the awful stench.

17 mins: Coach Mark shouts at the team. No one wants to go near the ball since it went in the hedge.

18 mins: Dazza comes on for Stevie.

19 mins: Dazza comes off, holding his stomach.

"It's growly so I can't run," moans Dazza.

Stevie is reading his book.

He refuses to go back on as well.

19 mins: Meerkats are playing the rest of the half with only five players.

None of them wants to touch the poopy ball.

Injury time: Pellie makes her first save – a miskick from the Sheepdogs striker.

She immediately sniffs her gloves to see if they've been pooped on.

A round of applause comes from the impressed parents.

Injury time: Bolo makes his first save too.

Unfortunately, Bolo is a defender and the ref whistles for a penalty with the ball sitting in Bolo's arms.

Injury time: Sheepdogs score the penalty.

11. HALF TIME

Coach Mark crouches in front of the team.

The Meerkats are happy because Coach Mark has swapped the match ball for a clean one.

He says: "You're doing really well. Excellent effort everyone.

"We could do a few things better.

"Remember passing? We haven't passed yet so that's something we can aim for.

"Pellie, brilliant save. Let's try and dive in the second half, shall we?"

Pellie still has the armband around her head.

"No," she replies, "it's too muddy."

Hildy slaps her friend on the back: "That's the best bit!"

Coach Mark moves to the rest of the team.

"Dazza and Stevie are coming back on so Hildy can have a rest."

"NOOOOO!"

Hildy is very upset.

She is COVERED in mud.

You cannot tell where the blue kit starts and ends. She is one big muddy blob.

Coach Mark gets strict.

"Yes, Hildy.

"Everyone has to be a sub at some point.

"You've been brilliant but the others need a chance too."

Stevie disagrees: "No, I don't want a chance.

"I want to sit here. I have a lot of important reading to catch up on."

Coach Mark says sternly: "No, you don't."

Stevie crosses his arms: "Yes, I do.

"You're wrong – my teacher says all the time that reading is super important.

"And I've reached a really good part in my book.

"It's too interesting to put down now."

Coach Mark: "The insects can wait, Stevie. On you go."

Stevie drops the book in shock.

Dribblers' eyes widen as he sees the book covered in mud.

Stevie begins to tremble.

The others move away from him.

Stevie has turned purple.

He screams at Coach Mark:

"THEY ARE NOT INSECTS. SPIDERS ARE ARACHNIDS! HOW DARE YOU!"

Coach Mark does not respond.

Instead he waves the team towards the pitch.

The Sheepdogs have taken up their positions ready for the restart.

The ref looks at the Meerkats.

Pellie walks to the goal, refusing to look in her mum's direction.

Bolo drags Stevie kicking and screaming to the pitch.

Dribbler inspects the new ball to ensure it does not have poop or sick on it. Dazza limps with one leg, then the other. Brendan is picking his nose.

Hildy is refusing to talk to Coach Mark on the sidelines.

Meerkats are ready.

12. SECOND HALF

21 minutes: 23–0.

22 mins: Stevie gives away the Meerkats' first-ever foul.

He kicks the Sheepdogs midfielder. He still looks mad after the spider/insect fiasco.

The referee gives Stevie a stern ticking off but Stevie stares towards Coach Mark.

Hildy, however, loves the terrible tackle and applauds Stevie wildly. Coach Mark does not.

23 mins: Dazza comes off with a hand injury.

Hildy goes on and runs straight over to Stevie to pat him on the back.

25 mins: 27–0.

27 mins: Meerkats get into the Sheepdogs' half for a second time, thanks to Stevie's huge toe-poke. Coach Mark is beginning to like Angry Stevie.

29 mins: Incredibly, Sheepdogs have not scored in FOUR minutes. And somehow Meerkats have managed to win a corner.

30 mins: 28–0.

31 mins: Pellie picks the ball up and kicks it long. It even goes out of the area.

Stevie does a flying karate kick to win the ball as the ball bounces.

He misses everyone by a whisker but the referee blows immediately for dangerous play. He tells Coach Mark to take Stevie off.

Stevie cheers.

Hildy is stunned and complains to the ref: "He didn't touch anyone.

"This is ridiculous."

"Any more nonsense from you, and you'll be off too," replied the ref.

Hildy storms off and gives the ref her best evil stare.

It's not a patch on Stevie's. In fact, Hildy looks like she's nibbled a bumblebee.

Dazza goes on, limping and holding his arm. Stevie sprints to the touchline, sits down and opens his book.

33 mins: 32–0.

34 mins: Dazza asks to come off. Coach Mark refuses.

35 mins: Hildy collapses onto the floor.

"I can't see, ref! Coach Mark – HELP ME! I'm blind."

The ref asks Coach Mark to come onto the pitch.

Hildy cannot open her eyes … because her face has too much MUD on it.

Coach Mark scrapes the dirt from her eyes.

Finally, Hildy's eyes, nose and mouth come into view.

She whispers: "They tried to stop me with mud, Coach Mark. Don't worry I won't give up."

Coach Mark has no idea what she's talking about.

36 mins: Hildy is running around the pitch trying to hack down Sheepdogs players, blaming them for the mud blinding.

37 mins: Gazza is slumped flat out in the Sheepdogs penalty area. No one knows why.

38 mins: There is CHAOS.

Several players are off the pitch among the crowd. One spectator has collapsed on the floor.

The ref is scratching her head and signals for Coach Mark to come over.

"Er, Coach Mark?

"I've never had this happen before?"

Coach Mark looks confused.

He jogs towards the ref.

"What's happened?

The ref replies: "The ball went out for a throw-in.

"An old chap kindly picked up the ball … and one of your team slide-tackled him."

Coach Mark groaned.

He knew who it was without even looking.

He leaves the ref and moves to the group of people gathered around the man.

Dazza's grandad is rolling on the floor clutching his leg.

"Ah, my ankle.

"She's broken it! I heard the snap."

Hildy stands over him, with both hands held up in front of her.

Splattered in mud, she looks delighted.

Hildy shakes her head: "It was a fair tackle.

"I can't help it if he's a diver."

Coach Mark slaps his forehead: "You're not supposed to tackle the crowd."

Hildy is shocked: "But I won the ball. I did exactly as you told me!"

Pellie arrives.

She agrees with Hildy.

"Yeah, Hildy did as you told her!"

Everyone looks at Coach Mark, shocked that he tells his team of children to attack supporters.

Dazza's grampa groans: "Has anyone called the hospital?"

Coach Mark tells Hildy off: "Tackles are supposed to happen on the pitch.

"Not off it! Right, you're coming off, young lady."

Hildy is puzzled: "What for?"

Coach Mark points at the man on the floor: "For hurting Dazza's grandad."

Hildy's mouth falls open: "For winning the ball cleanly?"

Dazza's grandad shouts: "I think I may lose this leg!"

Stevie appears out of nowhere: "A spider has eight legs.

"If you were a spider, you'd have seven legs left."

Dazza's grandad is getting angrier: "What on earth has a spider got to do with this?"

Stevie bursts into tears.

"WHY DOES EVERYONE HATE SPIDERS?"

Stevie's mum pushes in: "You've made my boy cry. You need to apologise."

Dazza's grandad pulls a face.

"Eh? My leg is almost broken here. Whom do you want me to apologise to?"

Stevie's mum points to Stevie: "To Stevie."

Stevie points to his book: "To the spiders."

Hildy points to herself: "To me.

"For trying to get me sent off. Are you a spy for the other team?"

Dazza's grandad waves a hand at Hildy: "You almost snapped my leg, young lady."

The referee checks her watch: "I need to restart the game.

"Can you please get off the pitch Coach Mark and make your substitution?"

Hildy stares at her: "I hate the ref."

Stevie joins in: "I hate Coach Mark."

Pellie agrees: "I hate my name."

39 mins: Hildy and Stevie are now off the pitch. Meerkats are down to five players again.

Well, four really.

Dazza is still lying in the Sheepdogs penalty area.

He's propped himself up to watch the game.

The bored Sheepdogs goalkeeper is chatting to him about crisps.

40 mins: 34–0.

Injury time: Dribbler gets the ball.

Since the hedge incident, he's barely had a touch.

He's tired.

Apart from Pellie, he's the only Meerkats player to play every single minute.

Football is hard work so Dribbler does something no one expected.

Dribbler passes.

Perhaps not a pass.

It's more of a long punt down the field.

Everyone stands still.

Dribbler doesn't pass or hit long balls.

Dribbler dribbles.
Except this time.

The ball flies deep into Sheepdogs' penalty area.

The Sheepdogs' keeper comes to grab the ball.

But he falls over Dazza's feet.

The ball sails over them both.

It rolls towards the goal … but thick mud stops it from crossing the goal line.

To everyone's disbelief, Dazza gets to his feet.

Everyone stops.

The ref.

Coach Mark.

Hildy.

Stevie.

All the parents. Every single player on the pitch.

It's Dazza on his own with the ball 30cm from an open goal.

He rushes towards the ball.

He slips and falls over.

His left leg connects with the ball at a funny angle.

Dazza collapses.

Everyone watching holds their breath. The ball shoots left.

It cannons onto the inside of the far post and dribbles along the goal line.

The Sheepdogs goalkeeper throws himself on top of Dazza to reach the ball at the last moment.

However the ball is out of reach.

It hits the other post.

And – somehow – trickles over the line.

Meerkats have scored.

GOAL!

They have done it.

Dazza has done it.

Against all the odds, the world's worst football team have scored a goal.

Full time:

Lane FC Meerkats U7s 1

Foxley Sheepdogs U7s 34

13. WE DID IT

Coach Mark stands in front of the Meerkats, who are flaked out on the floor.

"YOU DID IT.

"AMAZING. WELL DONE!"

The Meerkats look shocked.

Coach Mark is happy.

He is almost … excited. This is not normal.

Coach Mark claps his hands.

"Lane FC Meerkats – we are on the right path. No one can stop us now!"

THE END

ABOUT THE AUTHOR

Martin has advanced cystic fibrosis (CF) and lives with his wife, daughter and dog in the UK.

He writes children's books in his spare time while trying to stay away from football speculation and repeats of Top of the Pops.

His children's books include:

The Football Boy Wonder

The Demon Football Manager

The Magic Football Book

The Football Spy

The Football Superstar

The Football Boy Wonder Chronicles

The entire Charlie Fry Series is available via Amazon in paperback and Kindle today.

Follow Martin on:

Facebook
Facebook.com/footballboywonder

Instagram
@charliefrybooks

ABOUT THE ILLUSTRATOR

Philip Knibbs is an illustrator with a background in comic book artwork.

Based in Bedfordshire, he lives with his wife, two daughters, one dog, two cats, two rats, four foster squirrels and a giant African land snail.

You can keep up with what he's currently working on at
www.philbertz.com

COPYRIGHT

www.ingramcontent.com/pod-product-compliance
Lightning Source LLC
Chambersburg PA
CBHW031343060726
47590CB00007B/2605